The Gentleman
and the Kitchen Maid

by DIANE STANLEY

pictures by DENNIS NOLAN

Dial Books for Young Readers  New York

Illustrator's Note

In order to give full flavor to the artistic periods
depicted in this book, I researched the works of many painters.
Although no particular paintings were copied, various elements
were borrowed and general styles were employed for each subject.
The masters represented are:
Pablo Picasso, Claude Monet, Jan Vermeer, Pieter De Hooch,
Jacob van Ruisdael, Meyndert Hobbema, Jan van der Heyden, Frans Hals,
Rembrandt van Rijn, Gerard Ter Borch, Jan Cornelisz Verspronck,
Jan Steen, Willem van de Velde, Albert Cuyp, Abraham Van Beyeren,
Philips Wouwerman, Henri Rousseau, Amedeo Modigliani, and Marc Chagall.
The frames hang in the Yale Center for British Art,
and Rusty's palette follows the arrangement of pigments
suggested by James McNeill Whistler.
D.N.

Published by Dial Books for Young Readers
A Division of Penguin Books USA Inc.
375 Hudson Street
New York, New York 10014

Printed in Hong Kong
by South China Printing Company (1988) Limited
First Edition
1 3 5 7 9 10 8 6 4 2

Library of Congress Cataloging in Publication Data
Stanley, Diane.
The gentleman and the kitchen maid/
Diane Stanley; pictures by Dennis Nolan.
—1st ed. p. cm.
Summary: When two paintings hanging across from each other
in a museum fall in love, a resourceful art student
finds a way to unite the lovers.
ISBN 0-8037-1320-7—ISBN 0-8037-1321-5 (lib. bdg.)
[1. Painting—Fiction. 2. Museums—Fiction.]
I. Nolan, Dennis, ill. II. Title.
PZ7.S7869Ge 1994 [E]—dc20 93-157 CIP AC

The art was prepared using watercolors on watercolor paper.

For Nancy and Murray Bern,
friends indeed
D.S.

For Doug and Linda,
art lovers
D.N.

In the city there was a great art museum.

Every day of the week, from ten until six (and until nine on Thursdays), it opened its doors for the people of the city to come and look at the pictures.

Some walked quickly through the rooms and said, "Oh, Picasso!" (who was a famous painter), and went on to the next room to say, "Ah, Monet!" (who was another), and so on, without really noticing very much.

Others came to sit quietly looking at a favorite painting.

ROOM

12

Art students came with their brushes and paint to copy the work of the great masters, hoping to learn their secrets. One of these students was a tall girl with bright red hair. Her name was Rusty.

Rusty came there often. Sometimes she brought her friends and sometimes she came alone. On one particular Tuesday she climbed the steps at the entrance to the building, lugging an easel, a canvas, and a paint box.

She crossed the grand entrance hall and headed up another flight of stairs to the second floor. Then she wound her way through a maze of rooms to room twelve.

In room twelve hung a painting called "The Kitchen Maid." It showed a servant girl, just back from market, holding a basket of fruit. She stood looking over her shoulder, as if she had just heard the voice of a friend and was turning toward it. The artist who had painted her, a Dutch master, had lovingly rendered the fruit, the tile floor, the basket, the folds in the girl's dress, and the light shining on her fresh young face. Such a pretty picture it was!

Across from "The Kitchen Maid" hung "Portrait of a Young Gentleman." He was richly dressed in a satin jacket with a lace collar. His handsome face, framed by the long hair that men wore in those days, was so full of life and hope that it lifted one's spirits just to look at him. This artist (who was also Dutch) had painted him as if he had just stepped out from a shadow, with part of his face and hair lost in darkness.

These two paintings had hung across from each other for many years, and it happened that the gentleman and the kitchen maid had fallen in love.

But there they were, trapped in their different worlds, frozen in time. And what was worse, they had no privacy at all for their loving words and glances.

The bearded old man wearing a turban, whose portrait hung beside the gentleman's, advised him to forget her. She was not a real lady, he said.

"I can't imagine what he sees in her," commented the Grand Duchess with the large nose.

The stern gentleman in black believed the servant girl to be at fault for looking over her shoulder in such a pleasant way.

Even the little girl with pink cheeks thought the whole affair was just a lot of nonsense.

Only the men and women in the largest painting, who were eating roast meat and drinking beer (and had been having a fine time at it for over three hundred years), didn't care one way or the other.

This was the room Rusty entered on that Tuesday morning, just after opening time. She set up her easel in front of the young gentleman and began to work.

She was so absorbed in her painting, she forgot to eat lunch until after two o'clock. She bought a hot dog with sauerkraut from a street vendor and ate it on the steps of the museum. Then she hurried back to room twelve to begin the hardest part of the picture—the gentleman's face.

When she began to paint his eyes, she followed his longing gaze across the room. "Oh, I see what you're looking at!" she said out loud. "She *is* lovely. Just perfect for you!" And she chuckled quietly to herself as she painted.

Rusty was at work on the gentleman's hair when the guard began to flash the lights to announce closing time. She gathered up her things and left for the day.

The museum grew quiet.

"It's a pretty good likeness so far," commented the Duchess. "Better than the last one."

"I don't know why *you* get all the attention," muttered the stern man in black.

"She obviously has an eye for quality," said the gentleman, gazing longingly at his sweetheart.

"I do think it is going to be a very nice picture…" began the kitchen maid sweetly, when the little girl interrupted.

"Shhh! Someone's coming!"

"It must be rearranging time again," grumbled the man in the turban. "Why can't they ever make up their minds what goes where?"

The sound of footsteps and loud voices echoed through the empty museum, and a crowd of people came chattering into the room. While the directors directed, the guards watched, and the rest did all the lifting and carrying, "The Kitchen Maid" was taken down and moved to another room with Dutch paintings of a later period. In its place they hung a picture of fruit and goblets of wine arranged on a velvet drape.

When the room was quiet again, the little girl remarked that the fruit looked good enough to eat.

"And *that*," added the Duchess, "is an end to *that*!" and she glanced pointedly at the young gentleman.

Bright and early the next morning Rusty set up her easel and started to finish her painting. After a few minutes she put her brush down and looked from her copy to the gentleman and back again. She squinted and wrinkled her brow. "So sad!" she murmured. "Not like yesterday…"

Once again she followed his gaze across the room, and saw the glistening fruit. "Where is 'The Kitchen Maid'?" she asked the guard.

"Moved to room fourteen," he answered.

"Oh," she said, and stood there for a while looking at the gentleman and thinking. Then she began painting more quickly than the day before. She had only to finish his hair and one ruffled sleeve. She did not paint in all of the background.

"She didn't finish it," complained the little girl when Rusty had gone.

"She was probably bored with the subject," said the Duchess, who liked to have the last word.

Rusty hurried to room fourteen and began to paint "The Kitchen Maid"—not on a new canvas, but right into her painting of the young gentleman. His outstretched arm seemed to reach around her waist. She looked over her shoulder, into his eyes. They smiled at one another with perfect contentment.

Ever since that day, back in room twelve, the portrait of the gentleman has been silent. The object of criticism has now become the rowdy group in the largest painting. But they just ignore their critics, since they are having such a good time.

Rusty hung her picture in her favorite room at home. Everyone who has ever seen it thinks it is charming.

The other paintings in the room are quite modern and open-minded. Their conversation is stimulating and never unkind.

As for the gentleman and the kitchen maid, they will always be just as they are: stepping out into the sunshine together, their faces at once merry and tender. And who could ask for a happier ending than that?